Hurry Up, Henry

Jennifer Lanthier

Illustrations by Isabelle Malenfant

People were always telling Henry to hurry up.

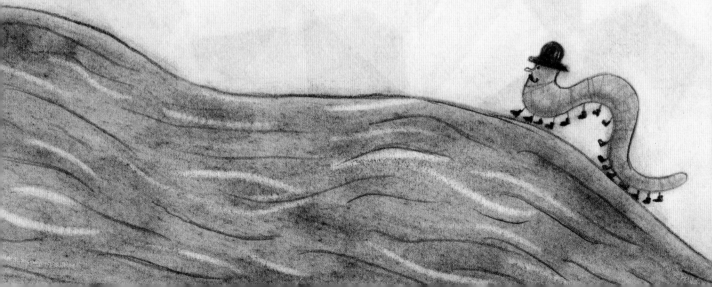

"Come on, Henry.
We're going to be late."

"We don't have time for
this, Henry.
We're going to be late."

"Hurry up, Henry. We're going to be late."

Henry didn't want to be late.

But he didn't want to hurry up, either.

Simon and Henry were best friends.
They lived in the same building and went
to the same school.

People were always telling Simon
to
slow
down.

When Simon came over, they got a lot done.

But once the elevator doors had closed
behind Simon, Henry would shut the blinds and
lie on the floor without moving.

Until it was time for supper.

**"Hurry up, Henry,
or I'll eat all the food."**

The only person who didn't seem to mind how slowly
Henry moved was Grandma. Grandma never hurried.

Sometimes she took more time than Henry.

If they needed to be somewhere at a certain time, Grandma made sure they got there.

They just left a little earlier.

The day before Henry's birthday,
Simon told Grandma he wanted to
make Henry the best present ever.
But he would need Grandma's help.

Grandma thought it was a good idea.

"One hour should do it."

The next day, everyone
gave Henry birthday hugs.
And then it was time
for school.

"Let's go, Henry."

"Hurry up, Henry."

"We're going to be late!"

But they weren't.

Today they had time.

Lots of time.

Lots and lots of time.

And nobody had to hurry.

"Thank you, Henry."

"Can we do this again tomorrow?"

To Lyla and Sam, Nicholas, Julia and Will — JL
To my sweet Alice, who lives in her own fantastic and timeless world — IM

PUFFIN

an imprint of Penguin Canada Books Inc., a Penguin Random House Company

Published by the Penguin Group

Penguin Canada Books Inc., 320 Front Street West, Suite 1400, Toronto, Ontario M5V 3B6, Canada

Penguin Group (USA) LLC, 375 Hudson Street, New York, New York 10014, U.S.A.

Penguin Books Ltd, 80 Strand, London WC2R 0RL, England

Penguin Ireland, 25 St Stephen's Green, Dublin 2, Ireland (a division of Penguin Books Ltd)

Penguin Group (Australia), 707 Collins Street, Melbourne, Victoria 3008, Australia
(a division of Pearson Australia Group Pty Ltd)

Penguin Books India Pvt Ltd, 11 Community Centre, Panchsheel Park, New Delhi – 110 017, India

Penguin Group (NZ), 67 Apollo Drive, Rosedale, Auckland 0632, New Zealand (a division of Pearson New Zealand Ltd)

Penguin Books (South Africa) (Pty) Ltd, 24 Sturdee Avenue, Rosebank, Johannesburg 2196, South Africa

Penguin Books Ltd, Registered Offices: 80 Strand, London WC2R 0RL, England

First published 2016

1 2 3 4 5 6 7 8 9 10

Text Copyright © Jennifer Lanthier, 2016
Illustrations copyright © Isabelle Malenfant, 2016

Manufactured in China

Library and Archives Canada Cataloguing in Publication

Lanthier, Jennifer, author
Hurry up, Henry / Jennifer Lanthier, Isabelle Malenfant.

ISBN 978-0-670-06837-1 (bound).--ISBN 978-0-14-319257-2 (paperback).--
ISBN 978-0-14-319258-9 (board book)

I. Malenfant, Isabelle, 1979-, illustrator II. Title.

PS8623.A69877H87 2016   jC813'.6   C2015-906991-2
American Library of Congress Cataloging in Publication data available

Visit the Penguin Canada website at www.penguinrandomhouse.ca

Penguin
Random
House